Inflation

by Martha London

Consultant: Emma Ryan, Social Studies Educator

BEARPORT
PUBLISHING

Minneapolis, Minnesota

Credits

Cover and title page, © Mehaniq/Shutterstock; 5T, © MuhsinRina/Shutterstock; 5B, © Gatot Adri/ Shutterstock; 7T, © Andrey_Popov/Shutterstock; 7B, © Odua Images/Shutterstock; 9, © AaronAmat/ iStock; 11, © Canadapanda/Shutterstock; 13T, © TarasM/Shutterstock; 13C, © Pushish Images/ Shutterstock; 13B, © Artashes/Shutterstock; 15, © Rido/Shutterstock; 17T, © bbernard/Shutterstock; 17B, © Pormezz/Shutterstock; 19, © Phillip Foster/Shutterstock; 21, © Tanarch/Shutterstock; 23, © YinYang/iStock; 25, © Everett Collection/Shutterstock; 26–27, © Monkey Business Images/ Shutterstock; 28T, © Kevin Dietsch/Getty Images; 28C, © Bloomberg/Getty Images; and 28B, © Bloomberg/Getty Images.

Bearport Publishing Company Product Development Team

President: Jen Jenson; Director of Product Development: Spencer Brinker; Senior Editor: Allison Juda; Editor: Charly Haley; Associate Editor: Naomi Reich; Senior Designer: Colin O'Dea; Associate Designer: Elena Klinkner; Product Development Assistant: Anita Stasson

Quote Sources

Page 28: John Barrasso from "U.S. Senate: Senate Session Part 2," *C-SPAN*, Feb. 15, 2022; Joe Biden from "The U.S. Economy Just Grew at Its Fastest Rate Since 1984," *Yahoo! News*, Jan. 27, 2022; Jerome Powell from "Here's What Jerome Powell's Second Term as Fed Chairman Means For Your Money," *CNBC*, Jan. 12, 2022.

Library of Congress Cataloging-in-Publication Data

Names: London, Martha, author.
Title: Inflation / by Martha London.
Description: Silvertip books. | Minneapolis, Minnesota : Bearport
  Publishing Company, [2023] | Series: In the news: need to know |
  Includes bibliographical references and index.
Identifiers: LCCN 2022008100 (print) | LCCN 2022008101 (ebook) | ISBN
  9798885091954 (library binding) | ISBN 9798885092029 (paperback) | ISBN
  9798885092098 (ebook)
Subjects: LCSH: Inflation (Finance)–Juvenile literature. |
  Economics–Juvenile literature.
Classification: LCC HG229 .L648 2023 (print) | LCC HG229 (ebook) | DDC
  332.41–dc23/eng/20220225
LC record available at https://lccn.loc.gov/2022008100
LC ebook record available at https://lccn.loc.gov/2022008101

For more information, write to Bearport Publishing, 5357 Penn Avenue South, Minneapolis, MN 55419. Printed in the United States of America.

Contents

Rising Prices

In 1970, a dozen eggs cost about 60¢. A men's haircut was about $5. Fifty years later, a dozen eggs cost closer to $2.50. The price of the haircut rose to more than $25. When prices go up over time, it's called inflation. Then, money can't buy as much as it did before.

Inflation affects both goods and services. Goods are things you buy, such as food. Services are things you pay someone to do for you. Getting a haircut is a service.

When costs rise, how do people still pay for things? During times of inflation, a company might sell something at a higher price. Then, they make more money. Over time, the company may pay its workers higher **wages**. This gives those people more money to buy things.

In 2000, the **average** wage was $14 per hour. In 2020, it was $24 per hour. This increase helped people keep up with rising prices.

Growth and Changes

A small amount of inflation usually means a country's **economy** is growing. Many people are working, which is good. They are getting paid enough to buy things. Costs of things go up as more people are spending.

Rising prices can change how people shop. People may want cheaper things to meet their needs. If the cost of beef goes up more than the cost of chicken, people may buy more chicken.

Reasons for the Rise

Prices often rise when the **demand** for something increases. In 2020, many people wanted face masks. The prices went up a lot.

Inflation can also happen when the **supply** of something gets smaller. If bad weather hurts orange trees, there may be less fruit. Then, the price of oranges increases.

Some **experts** think inflation is mostly caused by the amount of money in a country. When there is a lot of money to spend, prices go up.

Demand is often high for new items. People might line up to buy the latest phone.

Watching Costs

How do we measure inflation? One way is to look at the costs of basic things people need. These include food, electricity, and places to live. The way prices change over time shows us the **rate** of inflation.

The rate of inflation tells us how quickly or slowly costs rise. It also helps us understand how costs may affect a person or family.

Inflation and You

Sometimes, inflation rates rise very quickly. This can be hard for people. Suddenly, it takes more money to buy the same amount of something. People's wages may not catch up as fast. So, they can't buy as many things.

Between 2020 and 2021, inflation caused higher prices for several foods. The price of a pack of bacon went from $5.72 to $7.32. This was a big increase in a short time.

What about Wages?

It can be hard to tell if wages are keeping up with inflation. Over time, some items may become cheaper. Costs of other things could go up a lot. These differences can make it hard to see if wages are high enough to meet every person's needs.

In the United States, smartphones have become cheaper. But housing and healthcare costs have gone up. People with low wages may struggle to pay for a place to live or to see a doctor.

When It's Good

For some, inflation can be a good thing. Things gain **value**. For example, a person's home may become worth more over time. Then, if the person sells their home, they could get more money than they paid for it.

A little inflation can be good for the economy. When prices go up, it makes people spend more money. This gives companies extra money to make things and pay workers.

Inflation and Governments

Inflation happens all around the world. Each country's government works to control it. A country's economy only grows if people are buying and selling things. If prices rise too fast, people can't afford to buy things.

The Federal **Reserve** is the bank of the United States government. It works to reduce risks to the economy. Part of its job includes controlling the rate of inflation.

The U.S. Federal Reserve

A government may try to slow inflation in its country by raising **interest** rates. Interest is an extra amount that people must pay to banks or other places that **loan** them money. Higher interest rates mean people must pay more. They have less money to spend. This helps reduce demand and control inflation.

Governments decide how much money to put into a country at one time. This can also help control inflation. If there is too much money, inflation can rise too fast.

Going to Extremes

Sometimes, inflation becomes extreme. Hyperinflation (HYE-pur-in-FLAY-shun) is when prices rise at least 50 percent in a month. Something may suddenly cost $150 when it used to cost $100. Hyperinflation happens during war or other times of extreme change. While it is rare, it can make money in a country almost worthless.

Hyperinflation hurt Germany in the 1920s. People had buckets of money, but they still couldn't afford to buy bread.

Germany in the 1920s

Staying on Track

A little inflation will always be part of a healthy economy. However, things can go badly if inflation gets too high. That is why governments keep track of it. They work to make sure people can still afford things. Keeping inflation under control helps make the economy strong.

From 1991 until 2006, inflation in the United States stayed steady. Then, it dropped in 2008. Inflation was steady again throughout the 2010s. At the start of the 2020s, it went up again.

Voices in the News

People have many things to say about inflation. Some of their voices can be heard in the news.

John Barrasso
U.S. Senator

Right now, inflation is at a record high . . . prices in the United States [have] risen at their fastest pace in 40 years. 🙶

Joe Biden
President of the United States

🙶[Lowering healthcare and childcare costs] will address the biggest costs that working families face every day. 🙶

Jerome Powell
Chairman of the U.S. Federal Reserve

🙶We will use our tools to support the economy . . . and to prevent higher inflation. 🙶

★ SilverTips for REVIEW

Review what you've learned. Use the text to help you.

Define key terms

demand   supply

economy   wage

inflation

Check for understanding

What is inflation?

Describe one way that changes in supply and demand cause inflation.

Why do governments keep track of inflation?

Think deeper

How might inflation change the choices you make every day and over time?

★ SilverTips on TEST-TAKING

- **Make a study plan.** Ask your teacher what the test is going to cover. Then, set aside time to study a little bit every day.

- **Read all the questions carefully.** Be sure you know what is being asked.

- **Skip any questions** you don't know how to answer right away. Mark them and come back later if you have time.

Glossary

average the result of adding numbers together and dividing that amount by the number of total items

demand the amount that people want to buy something

economy the system of buying, selling, making things, and managing money in a place

experts people who know a lot about a certain subject

interest an extra amount of money paid for borrowing money

loan to let someone borrow money with plans for it to be paid back

rate an amount measured against a whole

reserve money kept safe to be used later

supply the amount of something there is available to buy

value how much money something is worth

wages money paid to people for working at jobs

Read More

Loria, Laura. *Inflation, Deflation, and Unemployment (Understanding Economics).* New York: Britannica Educational Publishing, 2019.

Pierce, Simon. *What's the Economy? (What's the Issue?).* New York: Kidhaven Publishing, 2022.

Ventura, Marne. *Supply and Demand (Community Economics).* Minneapolis: Abdo Publishing, 2019.

Learn More Online

1. Go to **www.factsurfer.com** or scan the QR code below.

2. Enter "**Inflation**" into the search box.

3. Click on the cover of this book to see a list of websites.

Index

About the Author

Martha London is a writer and educator in Minnesota. She lives with her cat.